MW00874908

This is a work based on Author's research and findings from various sources(especially; Internet).

About the Author

Sachin Sarkaniya is an Indian Author, who is a graduate of the University of Delhi and currently works for an Indian E-wallet company. As an author, Sachin has written multiple books in various genres.

Table of Content

The Quest for Treasure

Maya, an old woman, used to live in a small village. She was upset with her only son, Amit. At such an age, She had to work in the fields, throughout the day. Her son Amit, on the other hand, did not move a finger and never helped his mother in running their home.

Having taken breakfast, Amit would return home only at dinner time.
And Maya used to take care of both home and their small, ancestral farming land.
"When will you grow up?", Maya would often scold him and ask.

Most of the time, Maya remained ill and weak, but for Amit, wandering around the village was more important than his own mother's health. Days went by like this; Amit turned 25 years old, but his growing age did not impact his mood.
He was still a shirker and did not want to take responsibility.

One day, Maya returned home from the field. She was dead-tired, but somehow cooked dinner for the day. Amit came back and sat for dinner. *"My son, Look at me, I have grown old and weak. Lifting even a feather feels like moving a mountain now.*

I want you to come with me to the fields and help me", She said to him.

"Uhuh, Mother. I have no interest in working day and night at such an ugly place. I am devising a strategy to make quick money. I need some time, please don't force me to come with you", Amit bluntly replied.

Maya had tears in her eyes, but she did not oppose her son's idiotic answer. A few days later, Maya's cousin Reena, visited her home to meet her. "You look weaker than before", Reena worriedly said. "Oh, that's nothing. I have grown old. These are just the signs of my old age. Hahaha!", Maya tried to cover up. "Don't lie, Maya, I know you are under stress", Reena quickly said to her.

Maya, with a heavy heart, narrated about her troubles and her lazy son to her cousin. *"Hmmm, I think I can fix it easily"*, Reena smiled at her and said, and she whispered something in Maya's ears.

The next day, After having Breakfast, Amit was about to leave outside, and when suddenly, an old piece of paper near the mirror, got his attention. When he read it, he curiously asked his mother, *"Where did this paper come from?"*.

"Oh, my son. Light night, A fairy had come to our home. She was thirsty and needed some water. I gave her some water and in return, The fairy handed over this piece of paper to me. By the way, what's that in the paper?", Maya said.

"Mother, It's a map of treasure, and as per this map, there lies a hidden treasure

in our fields. Let's go and find out", And Amit, like the speed of electricity, picked up a shovel, some other tools and rushed towards their fields.

For the next 3 days, He kept digging the fields. His mother Maya, was happy that finally, her son had started working and helping her. But even after 3 days, Amit did not even get a small metal piece in the fields; let alone a box of treasure. He was frustrated and wanted to go back home.

Maya stopped him and requested, *"Son, since you now have dug up the entire field, Why don't you place seeds and finish it completely?"*

Amit had no energy left to resist. He spread the seeds and returned home completely exhausted; for the very first time in his life. A few days later, Amit was combing his hair.

He again found a piece of white paper near to the mirror. *"I am sorry for the incomplete information. In return for your kindness old lady, I would like to gift you diamonds. For that, You need to harvest your crops. Once you have done so, Just say, "little magical fairy, where are my diamonds! And your diamonds will appear out of your fields"*

Amit ran towards his mother and inquired about the note. *"That same fairy had come again last night. She did not say anything but just apologized for something and gave me a piece of paper. Now, my eye-sight is weak and I cannot read what is written in the note"*, Maya told him.

Amit, being blind by a quick money scam, rushed towards their fields and started harvesting all alone. It took him an entire day to cut the crops and place them in the tractor, so that they could be sent to the market.

Maya by now had reached the fields along with her cousin, Reena. Amit was so obsessed with diamonds that he did not eat lunch either that day.

Finally, when the fields were once again barren and empty, He excitedly spoke the magical spell, *"Little magical fairy, where are my diamonds!"*

But there was no movement on the ground. He repeated the words, "*Little magical fairy, where are my diamonds!* but this attempt was in vain too.

He suddenly heard someone's laughter- his mother and aunt were laughing loudly. Amit realized that he was tricked. Maya came closer to him and narrated everything from the very beginning, "*There is no treasure or diamonds in our fields. It was your aunt, who suggested to me this plan. No fairy had come to our home*".

"*But, I had seen the map myself*", Amit replied in amazement. "*Oh, that map. Reena had drawn that map and placed it next to the mirror. Reena also wrote the second letter of the fairy"*, and both Reena and Maya laughed again.

Amit was angry to have been deceived. *"Listen my son. There is your treasure"*, Maya showed him, pointing towards the tractor. *"Sell this crop in the market and you will earn a huge profit. And never be afraid of hard work anymore"*, She continued.

Amit went to the market and sold crops. He earned a handsome profit on the sale. From that day, Amit became more responsible and started looking after their ancestral fields. He would wake up early, reach the fields, and work there round the clock. Upon selling crops to the dealers, he would give the entire money to his mother.

Maya was now free from worries, as her shirker son, had now become wise and responsible.

She would often write thank you letters to her cousin Reena, for helping her.

The Lion and The Mouse

Max the mouse loved roaming in the forest and playing mischief on other animals. He would intertwine the snake's long tail, make a hole in the sparrow's net, and sometimes, dug a tiny canal towards the ant's colony.

Animals of that forest often complained about him to his parents, but that did not stop Max from teasing others.

One day, Max was strolling in the jungle; in search of something interesting. It was afternoon time, and most of the animals remained in their homes. The small mouse looked around, but he seemed to be the only one, who did not rest that day.

Suddenly, He saw the king of the jungle, Lion.

The Lion had just eaten lunch and was sleeping out of the open. Max sneakily walked towards him. After examining for a while, he realized that the lion was in deep sleep. *"I can now have fun"*, the mouse whispered.

He quickly climbed on the lion's back and started jumping. He then went through his long hair and relaxed there for a while; as if it were a soft bed.

After that, Max ran towards his tail and slid down the ground. *"This is awesome"*, He screamed joyously. The little mouse would climb on the lion and slide down over his tail.

The Lion woke up & roared, *"Who dared to disturb me"*, he angrily asked and looked around. The little mouse jumped forward and introduced himself, *"Your highness. I was the one who was playing over you"*.

"You little mouse, You awoke me. Don't you know i am the king of this jungle? Today is your last day on earth. Now be ready to get eaten", and the cruel lion caught the mouse in his paw.

Max was very scared; He was trembling with fear and pleaded to the lion, *"Oh great king of the jungle. I know I should not have bothered you while you were asleep. I truly apologize for my mischief. I beg you to spare my life. Even though I* am very small, I will surely help you one day- in every way possible".

"Hahaha! How can someone as little as you, help the king of the jungle? The Lion laughed.
Anyway, You are lucky that I have taken lunch. Now go and never come near to my lair", and the lion released the mouse. Max thanked him for his kindness and rushed towards his home.

A few days went by; The Jungle was flourishing. There was no scarcity of food, water, and safe shelter. As a result, animals of the other jungle started coming there. A group of hunters heard about the prosperity and abundance of animals in this jungle.

One day, the group of hunters sneakily entered the jungle and started catching animals. They managed to imprison hyenas, monkeys, and a few bears, but their main motive was to catch and take away the king of the jungle, Lion.

The wisest of hunters suggested placing a strong and unbreakable net below a tree. On the net, Fresh flesh was left to tantalize the lion.

Sniffing the fresh flesh, the lion reached the spot and got caught in the net. He tried to break the net and cut its strings, but nothing worked. His sharp paws had no impact on the net, either.

Now, Lion was in serious trouble; the hunters would come anytime and kill him.

He could see his death now. While Lion was sitting helplessly, He heard someone's squeak. Max the mouse, was cutting strings of the net one by one with the help of his sharp front teeth.

After some time, he managed to tear apart a large portion of the net, and the lion quickly came out through the hole.

The mouse rode on the lion and they both fled towards the safest place. The Lion was now out of danger. He thanked the mouse and asked him, *"How did you know I was captured by the hunters. I remember I had warned you not to come around my lair"*.

"Your highness, I respect your commands and did not want to disoblige. But when I

was going towards the river, I saw humans, who seemed hunters to me. I went back home and told everything to my father.

He said that hunters usually capture lions and other giant animals. I thought your life would be in danger. You had once spared my life, and it was time for me to return your favor", the mouse narrated everything to the lion. The Lion thanked him once again, and from then on, they became very close friends.

The Selfish Burger-seller

The Tale begins in a small village. There lived a woman who used to make the best and most delicious burger. She would make burgers by the afternoon, and roam around the village with her small go-cart; selling burgers.

Since people loved her burger, she did not need to worry about customers and would make a decent profit by selling burgers. She had a son and a daughter.

Years went by, She had grown old and most of the time, used to remain ill. It had now become difficult for her to make burgers, and sell them in the village.

A few weeks later, She died. During her last days, She had taught her daughter, Marry the process of making burgers.

Marry too, was fond of cooking, and learnt the art from her mother.After her death, Both Marry and her brother, Jacob, were in trouble. Their only source of income was their mother's business.

"Should we continue our mother's business?" Asked Jacob, having made unsuccessful attempts to get a job.

"We can try once. I can prepare burgers", She said. *"Alright, I am a people person, and i can sell those burgers in the village"*, Jacob suggested.

The next day, Marry went to the market and bought raw materials for the burgers.

By afternoon, she ended up making 25 burgers. Jacob laid them on the cart, and went outside to sell the burgers. A few passersby bought burgers and praised its taste.

Before sunset, Jacob had succeeded in selling all the burgers and happily returned home to show his sister the money he had earned. Marry was happy, too, that people liked her burgers.

From that day onwards, their business took off and never saw any downfall. Marry would make tasty burgers, and Jacob would cajole people and sell lots of burgers daily.

Jacob and marry divided profit equally between them. Their life was on track and the future seemed bright and safe. But being a human, Jacob was not satisfied with the share of profit he received. *"I know how to talk to people and persuade them to buy burgers.*

Moreover, I also roam around the village the entire day and get tired completely. I have been working very hard to run this business. Thus, I deserve more profit", Jacob mumbled in frustration.

Later that day, he went back home and discussed the matter with his sister, Marry. *"Look, Jacob. I know you work a lot. But that does not mean you will get more share in the profit. I, too, work round the clock. I go to the market, buy* raw materials, then make burgers from morning to afternoon", Marry firmly said to him.

"I don't agree with you. Cooking these burgers does not take so much effort. My work is more important and tiresome than yours", Jacob replied.

The Argument kept going and finally, Jacob decided to quit the partnership. Marry tried to make him understand, but he did not want to compromise with the profit share.

The next day, Jacob brought raw materials and started making burgers. He was delighted that now, all the profit would go into his pocket only. From morning to afternoon, He prepared buns, sauce, and stuffing for the burgers.

By afternoon, he was ready to sell them in the village, but he was exhausted. Jacob strolled with his cart in the village. Since people already loved the burgers he used to sell, They went to him and bought burgers.

After having a small bite, A man complained, *"What's this Jacob. Have you forgotten to add spices?"* *"This burger is very insipid"*, another customer said bitterly. *"I am very sorry gentlemen. It seems I had forgotten to add enough spices.*

I promise that from tomorrow on, The burgers will be as tasty and spicy as I used to make earlier", Jacob apologized and gave them assurance.

The next day, He made burgers and went out to sell them, but today, he had no energy to roam in the village and sell burgers.

The process of making burgers was grinding and took hours. But somehow, Jacob began selling burgers. Again, customers were not happy with the inferior taste of his burgers.

He realized that his plan had failed, and he was doomed from both ends; First, the quality of the burgers was below average, and second, since Jacob was handling everything himself, He used to be tired all day.

"I am such an idiot. I should not have been so greedy. My sister was right. She indeed worked hard for our burger's business"
Jacob repented
for his greediness and swore that he would never become so greedy.

The Crow and the Snake

Once upon a time, there was a jungle in the kingdom of emperor Ashoka. The Jungle was very prosperous and there used to live a lot of animals.

On the east side of that same jungle, near the river, there was a mango tree. On that tree, A Crow used to live with his eggs.

A nasty snake troubled him a lot; He would sneakily enter his nest when the crow was outside, and eat all his eggs.

The Crow tried to make him understand and requested many times, not to eat his eggs, but the snake was too dangerous to argue with. *"Do what you want.*

I will be eating your eggs as long as I want. After all, these are very delicious", The Snake laughed and said to him.

A few days went by like this, The Crow had to fly around the jungle for food and water. Meanwhile, the snake would come to his nest and make off with his eggs. He returned and found some eggs missing, and knew who was behind this. He wanted to get rid of that evil snake; anyhow.

There lived a wise parrot in the jungle, who happened to be his close friend. The Crow went to him and told him his problem. The wise parrot thought for a while and smiled at him, *"You don't need to worry anymore, My friend.*

That evil snake is not going to eat your eggs and harm you in any way", he said to the Crow. *"But how"*, Asked Crow desperately. *"Tomorrow, in the morning, go to the river.*

There, the princess comes with her friends to bathe. Before going inside the river, they keep their belongings and jewelry on a stone. Just steal away her necklace and throw it inside the snake's home".

"Sorry my dear friend, but i don't understand what will happen by this?", the crow asked him once again. *"Just do as I say"*, assured the parrot. The next day,

The Crow went to the river and picked up the princess's necklace in his beak.

The Guards of the princess saw him and ran towards the crow, but he quickly flew off the ground. The Guards followed the crow until he reached the snake's home.

The Crow threw the necklace inside the evil snake's home and escaped before the guards could catch him. The Guards surrounded the snake's home and started digging it.

Due to this commotion, the snake came out of home, and one of the guards screamed, *"Hey look, here is the snake. He is very venomous and may kill us.*

And the guards hit him with the sticks and spares. They kept beating the snake until he died. They recovered the necklace from his home and returned to the river.

The Crow was watching all this over a tree and sighed with relief. He went towards the parrot's home; to thank him.

Mathew: The Milkshake Man

On the west coast of the Thames River, there was a town, which was famous for its Milkshake. A man named Mathew used to prepare the best milkshake people had ever tested. He loved making milkshakes and wanted to do this for the rest of his life.

Though Mathew's shop was not as big and classy, people would come from various towns and villages- to enjoy his tasty milkshake. *"You are the best Mathew. When i drink your milkshake, it feels as if the Gods of the paradise themselves made this milkshake"*, one of the customers said, while sipping the chilled glass of milkshake.

"No, No. I think Mathew knows some sort of magic and uses it to make such tasty milkshakes, Another customer laughed and said. "Brother Mathew, Please pack three glasses as well for take-away. I want my family to taste your delicious milkshakes", A man placed the order, while drinking his milkshake.

Mathew's life was going smoothly, and he was content with the little he earned by selling milkshakes. One day, a man came to his shop and ordered a glass of milkshake.

After finishing the milkshake, He praised Mathew and said, "How tasty this milkshake was! Thank you so much dear

Mathew. I have never tasted such a delicious drink in my life"

Mathew smiled and thanked him. *"But, if you don't mind, i want to say something. Something was missing"*, the man hesitantly said.

Mathew looked at him and waited for him to complete. *"I have been to town many times.*

There, the big restaurants serve milkshakes along with Ice-cream. It enhances the taste of milkshakes. Why don't you sell Ice-cream as well? People who come for your milkshakes will also start buying ice-cream from you, and you will be earning double profit", The man suggested.

"Hmmm, that's not a bad idea. But i don't know how to make ice cream", Mathew told him. "You don't worry at all, I know a man in my town, who makes very delicious ice-cream. I will come with him tomorrow", the man said to him and left for his home.

The next day, the man returned to Matthew's shop and introduced him to a man, who was somewhat small in height. "This is my friend James. He is the best ice-cream maker around". They set up a small stall next to Mathew's milkshake stall and James started selling ice-cream.

Since Mathew was very famous in the town, whoever came for his milkshake, also bought ice-cream from James.

People now started drinking milkshakes with Ice-cream. It indeed enhanced the taste of Matthew's milkshake, and Mathew was now making more money than before. The Idea of an Ice-cream milkshake was a massive success. James, like Mathew, loved cooking, and requested Mathew to teach him the process of making milkshakes.

Mathew helped his friend and taught him the entire process of making delicious milkshakes. Their business was growing day by day and it used to be difficult for both James and Mathew to handle so many customers.

One day, James did not show up at the stall. Mathew waited for him that day, but he did not come. *"James must be ill or may have stuck into an emergency"*, He thought. A few more days went by but there was no information about James.

By this time, Mathew started losing customers. People had become used to ice-cream milkshakes. Since James was not there anymore, there was no ice-cream available, and unfortunately, Mathew did not know how to make ice-cream, either. Customers would come and ask for an Ice-cream milkshake, and return empty-handed.

Mathew was unable to sell even a single glass of milkshake. He was upset and did not know what to do next. One day, his friend Allen visited his shop to meet him.

Allen inquired how his milkshake business was. *"What do I tell you, friend? My business has come to zero. People only want an Ice-cream milkshake"*, Mathew sadly told him.

Allen said to him, *"There is a very famous shop in the town across the river. It's very famous for its ice-cream milkshake. Let's go and see"*

Allen and Mathew went to the town to see that shop. There, customers were standing in long queues, just to buy ice-cream milkshake. The Shop seemed to be earning huge profits. Suddenly, Mathew looked at the owners of the shop.

It was James, who was making ice-cream at one stall, and next to him, the man who suggested Mathew the idea of ice-cream and milkshake, was selling milkshakes. Mathew realized that he was duped by this man and his business partner, James.

Actually, they wanted to learn from Mathew how milkshakes are made, so that they could sell both ice-cream and milkshakes, and acquire all the customers- and ultimately, make more money.

Mathew was angry, but what could be done here? *"I should not have trusted a stranger"*, he mumbled to himself. And with a heavy heart, he returned to his town along with Allen.

The Monkey and The Crocodile

Once upon a time, There lived a Crocodile in the river of the African Forest. He was once a cruel and clever predator, but now, had grown older, and due to his old age, He was not able to hunt. The Crocodile's name was Josh.

At the end of the river, there was a vast tree of mulberries, and on that same tree, Mickey the monkey lived. The monkey always ate tasty and sweet mulberries and would jump from one branch to another.

His life was full of joy. On the other hand, Josh the Crocodile had to remain hungry for days. One day, Josh saw Mickey, lying on a branch, and chewing mulberry.

He said to the monkey, *"Hey Little Monkey. I have been very hungry for days. Would you please give me some mulberries to eat"*?

The Monkey was very kind and could not resist his request. He climbed up the tree, and plucked mulberries for the Crocodile. *"Here are your mulberries"*, Mickey said while giving him some mulberries. Josh looked at the mulberries for a while and felt something strange.

Since Crocodiles are carnivores, Josh had not eaten such a thing in his life. *"You may eat them, You are not gonna die"*, Laughed the monkey and said to him.

The Crocodile ate the mulberries and stood like a statue for a moment. He had never tasted such a delicious thing.

"*Wow, these mulberries are indeed very sweet and tasty*", He said to the monkey. From that day onwards, The Crocodile would come out of the water, and ask mickey for mulberries.

Mickey too loved sharing mulberries with him. They had now become friends.

Mickey and Josh used to play with each other. He would hop on Crocodile, and roam around the river. Sometimes, Mickey gave him a head massage.
With the passage of time, their friendship grew stronger.

The Crocodile thought to gift his wife mulberries. He requested the monkey if he could give him some mulberries. The Monkey quickly climbed through the branches, plucked some mulberries, and gave them to the Crocodile.

"Thank you, my friend. I owe you this", and The Crocodile went back to his home. He showed mulberries to his wife. She ate the mulberries and said," These mulberries are so tasty and sweet. I was thinking if these mulberries are as sweet, then how sweet that monkey's heart will be, who daily eats such sweet mulberries?"

"Dear, I did not get your point", Asked Josh in confusion. "I want you to bring me *that monkey's heart"*, She revealed her evil intentions and told him. *"But, But, The Monkey is my friend. I remember he helped me and saved my life when I had nothing to eat. I cannot deceive him like this"*, Josh firmly said.

"I don't wanna hear anything. I just want to eat his tasty heart. Bring it to me anyhow. It has been a long time since I ate flesh. And if you don't bring him here, I will never talk to you again, She said to him.

"But how will i bring him here?", asked Josh. *"Just Invite him for lunch today and bring him here, and I will take care of rest"*, She instructed Josh.
Josh reluctantly agreed. He went back to meet the monkey and called out for him.

Mickey appeared from one of the branches and asked him, *"So, what should we play today?"*. *"Actually, Today, My wife has prepared tasty food that you love, and she has invited you for lunch today"*, The Crocodile told him. *"Alright, I will come with you"*, And the monkey sat on Josh's back.

The Crocodile swam through the river towards his home. The Monkey was curious to know what his wife had cooked for lunch. *"She has cooked sweet rice, banana shake, mango curry, and fresh jam with the mulberries you gave me yesterday"*, He told Mickey.

Mickey was drooling when he imagined such delicious dishes. Meanwhile, Josh felt bad for his friend and mumbled to himself. *"I am deceiving my friend. I think i should tell him the truth"*. *He once helped me when I was about to starve"*.

"My dear friend mickey. I wanted to say something", He hesitantly said. *"Yes my friend, Tell me what's that?"* The Monkey excitedly asked. *"We have not planned any lunch. My wife wanted to eat your heart.*

She said it would be very tasty. I requested her not to do so, but she warned me that she would never talk to me if I did not give her your heart". The Monkey was shocked by his words and wanted to jump off his back to save his life. But they were in the center of the river, and there was deep water all around.

"Is this all you want? You are not my friend. Friends share everything with each other. Ok, let it be. You should have told me that your wife wanted to eat my heart. I would keep it in my pocket before coming here.

Now, what should I do?", The Monkey said to him and pretended as if nothing had happened. "So, where is your heart now?", Asked The crocodile curiously.

"We monkeys keep jumping here and there. Therefore, We keep our heart safe on the branch; lest it may fall.

Now, We will have to go back and collect my heart", Mickey told him. "No problem, I will swim quickly and get back to your home and we will bring your heart for my wife", said the crocodile.

"What can we do else?", replied the monkey. The Crocodile swam as fast as he could and reached the shore of the river, where the monkey lived.
As soon as the monkey saw dry land, He jumped off his back and speedily climbed up the tree.

"Now I am safe", He sighed in relief and said angrily to the Crocodile, "You are an idiot. How can someone remain alive without his heart. You have proved that you are not trustworthy. I had helped you when you needed food to eat. But you deceived me. Now, Go to hell".

And the monkey began swinging towards the other part of the jungle so that the deceitful Crocodile could never find him again.

The Farmer and the Storm

Once upon a time, in a far, remote village-
there lived a farmer, who had a mid-sized
agricultural land, a tiny farm wherein
there were a bunch of cattle and their
shelter in which, the farmer would tether
all of them at night. His Village was
notorious for heavy storms, cyclones that
frequently occurred around where his
fields were located. Thus, He was not able
to find anyone to work for him. Trying his
luck, he eventually gave an advertisement
in the newspaper and as a result, A gaunt,
not-so-tall guy arrived at his place for the
interview. The man laid one condition
before the farmer- *"I do not work when
the wind blows"*, He firmly said.

Since the farmer did not have any option, he hired him on the spot. Few months went by with peace. But one day, as it was expected, the cyclone showed up at the village. The farmer rushed to his fields, where the man used to live in a small shed. He awoke him up and thundered at him, *"You are asleep, stupid. The cyclone is around the corner."* The man did not budge an inch. Rather, he kept lying on his cot as if nothing had happened, and replied with ease, *"Remember What I had told you, I do not work when the wind blows."*

The farmer realized that he had made a mistake appointing him as the keeper. But the need of the hour was to protect his fields, cattle, and machinery. So, he sped outside to protect what he could. But to his amazement, everything was already in safe hands; the cattles were tightly-tethered inside their shelter, crops reaped by the man were covered with a sturdy tarpaulin that would easily withstand the deadly cyclone. The Farmer went back to the small shed and looked at the man for a while. He started walking towards his home; With a smile of having learned a life-long lesson, that would help him survive any kind of cyclones of life. The moral of the story:- Do not wait until it is too late to regret. Always be prepared for the future, and for that, You will have to come into discipline mode. The man had the discipline; to get the most important work done every day- and so must we, so that when the wind blows, we can rest too.

THANK YOU NOTE

THANK YOU FOR READING THIS BOOK

IF YOU LIKED THIS BOOK, PLEASE
TELL US AND SHARE YOUR REVIEW ON
AMAZON.

PLEASE ALSO CHECK below books By the
AUTHOR

7 Interesting Small Stories With Morals
For Kids: Best Moral Stories in English &
Nighttime Stories For Kids

Hard Riddles Book for Smart Kids: 400
Difficult Riddles, Crime riddles, Brain
Teasers & Funny Riddles for Kids to
Become Smarter

Interesting English Fairy Tale Stories: Amazing Stories, Fantasy Fairy Tale and Night Time Stories Book For Kids

Millionaire Habits Book: How to be More Productive, Self Controlled and Go After Your Dreams || Habits of Highly Successful People

Her Betrayal: A Broken Heart Romance Novel Based On Real Life Story Of A Young Boy And His Inspiring Journey Towards Realization About Life

Made in the USA
Las Vegas, NV
03 May 2024

89486932R00039